WITHDRAWN

W9-BEB-594

FORTUNATELY

Written and illustrated by
REMY CHARLIP

Four Winds Press   New York

Library of Congress Cataloging in Publication Data

Charlip, Remy.
  Fortunately.
  Reprint of the ed. published by Parents' Magazine Press, New York.
  Summary: Good and bad luck accompany Ned from New York to Florida on his way to a sur-
prise party.
  [1. Luck — Fiction] I. Title.
[PZ7.C3812Fo 1980] [E] 80-36956 ISBN 0-590-07762-7

PUBLISHED BY FOUR WINDS PRESS. A DIVISION OF SCHOLASTIC MAGAZINES,
INC., NEW YORK, N.Y. COPYRIGHT © 1964 BY REMY CHARLIP. ALL RIGHTS RE-
SERVED. PRINTED IN THE UNITED STATES OF AMERICA. LIBRARY OF CONGRESS
CATALOG CARD NUMBER: 80-36956. 1 2 3 4 5 84 83 82 81 80

THIS BOOK IS DEDICATED TO NED AND CLAUDE AND THE PAPER BAG PLAYERS

Fortunately
one day, Ned got a letter that said,
"Please Come to a Surprise Party."

Fortunately
a friend loaned him an airplane.

Unfortunately
the motor exploded.

Fortunately
there was a parachute in the airplan

***Unfortunately*
*there was a hole in the parachute.***

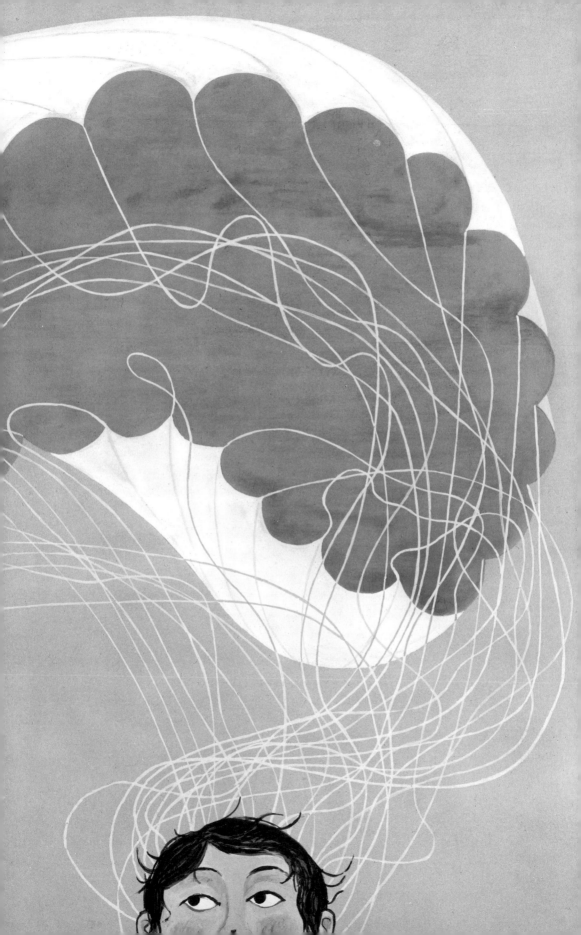

Fortunately
there was a haystack on the ground.

**Unfortunately
there was a pitchfork in the haystack.**

Fortunately
he missed the pitchfork.

Unfortunately
he missed the haystack.

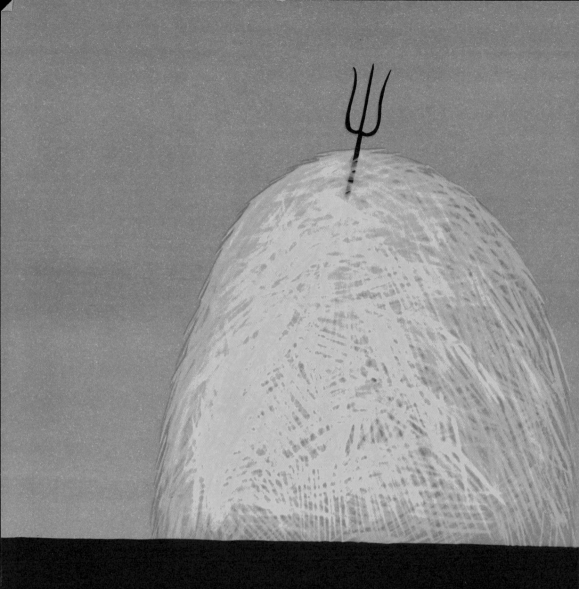

**Fortunately
he landed in water.**

Unfortunately
there were sharks in the water.

Fortunately
he could swim.

Unfortunately
there were tigers on the land.

**Fortunately
he could run.**

Unfortunately
he ran into a deep dark cave.

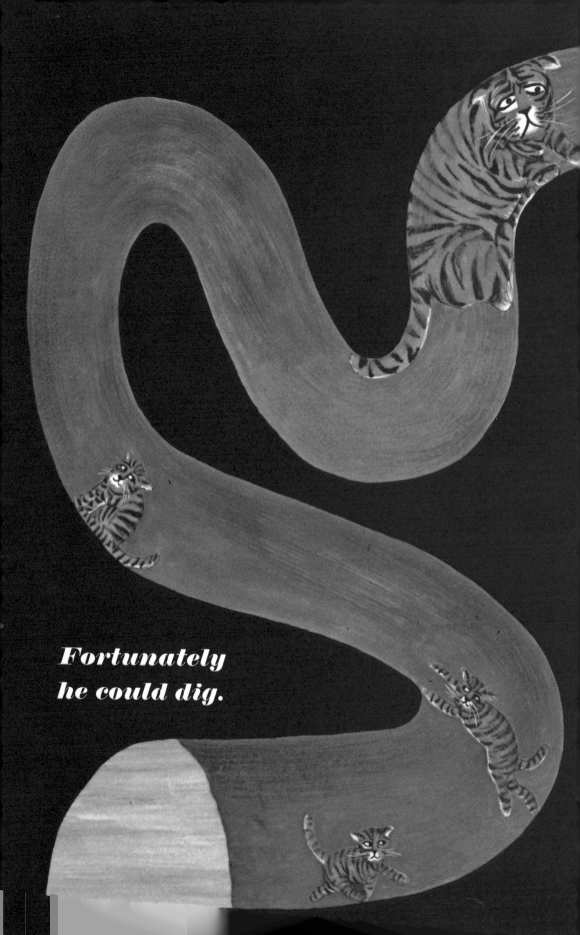

*Fortunately
he could dig.*

Unfortunately
he dug himself into a fancy ballroom.

Fortunately
there was a surprise party going on.
And fortunately
the party was for him,
because fortunately
it was his birthday!

4